Dear Parent:
Your child's love of reading starts here!

Every child learns to read in a different way and at his or her own speed. Some go back and forth between reading levels and read favorite books again and again. Others read through each level in order. You can help your young reader improve and become more confident by encouraging his or her own interests and abilities. From books your child reads with you to the first books he or she reads alone, there are I Can Read Books for every stage of reading:

SHARED READING
Basic language, word repetition, and whimsical illustrations, ideal for sharing with your emergent reader

BEGINNING READING
Short sentences, familiar words, and simple concepts for children eager to read on their own

READING WITH HELP
Engaging stories, longer sentences, and language play for developing readers

READING ALONE
Complex plots, challenging vocabulary, and high-interest topics for the independent reader

ADVANCED READING
Short paragraphs, chapters, and exciting themes for the perfect bridge to chapter books

I Can Read Books have introduced children to the joy of reading since 1957. Featuring award-winning authors and illustrators and a fabulous cast of beloved characters, I Can Read Books set the standard for beginning readers.

A lifetime of discovery begins with the magical words "I Can Read!"

Visit www.icanread.com for information
on enriching your child's reading experience.

I Can Read Book® is a trademark of HarperCollins Publishers.
Flat Stanley and the Missing Pumpkins
Text copyright © 2017 by the Trust u/w/o Richard C. Brown f/b/o Duncan Brown.
Illustrations by Macky Pamintuan, copyright © 2017 HarperCollins Publishers.
All rights reserved. Manufactured in China.
www.icanread.com
Library of Congress Catalog Card Number: 2016952957
ISBN 978-0-06-236598-9 (trade bdg.)—ISBN 978-0-06-236594-1 (pbk.)
Typography by Jeff Shake

17 18 19 20 21 SCP 10 9 8 7 6 5 4 3 2 1   ❖   First Edition

I Can Read!

READING WITH HELP 2

FLAT STANLEY

and the
Missing Pumpkins

created by Jeff Brown

by Lori Haskins Houran

pictures by Macky Pamintuan

HARPER

An Imprint of HarperCollinsPublishers

Stanley Lambchop lived
with his mother, his father,
and his little brother, Arthur.

Stanley was four feet tall,

about a foot wide,

and half an inch thick.

He had been flat ever since

a bulletin board fell on him.

"Ow! Your flat elbow is so pointy!"
said Arthur.

Stanley and Arthur were squashed
in the backseat of the car.

"Sorry," Stanley said.

He folded himself up like a taco

so his elbow wouldn't poke Arthur.

"Better?" he asked.

"Better," said Arthur.

The boys were on their way
to their cousin Billy's farm.
"I envy you," Mrs. Lambchop said.
"Two weeks of fresh air.
And the county fair!"

"I can't wait to see Billy!"

said Arthur.

"And Aunt Sue and Uncle Bob,"

said Stanley.

Aunt Sue was always baking pies

to fatten him up.

"I'm flat, not skinny," he'd tell her.

It didn't seem to matter.

The Lambchops pulled up
to a big red farmhouse.

"BILLY!" yelled Arthur.

"ARTHUR!" yelled Billy.

They took off together.

"Don't get into trouble!"

Mrs. Lambchop called after them.

Stanley said good-bye to his parents.

Uncle Bob helped with the bags.

"Ready for some chores?"

Uncle Bob asked.

"You bet!" Stanley said.

Stanley loved doing farm chores.

He was good at it, too.

He could slide his flat hands

under the hens to collect their eggs.

They didn't mind a bit!

Stanley could slip his flat body

between rows to get every ear of corn.

"Best picker around," said Uncle Bob.

And when Uncle Bob needed to unload
hay bales from his truck,
Stanley made the perfect ramp.

"You're mighty helpful, Stanley,"

Uncle Bob said one night at dinner.

"But you are still so thin!"

said Aunt Sue.

"Even with all my good cooking!

You MUST eat another slice of pie."

After dessert,

Stanley went with Uncle Bob

to fix a scarecrow

in the pumpkin patch.

"This scarecrow does a fine job scaring off birds," Uncle Bob said. "Too bad it can't scare off thieves. Someone's been taking my pumpkins."

"That's awful!" said Stanley.

"And right before the county fair!"

"Oh, I never show my pumpkins
at the fair," Uncle Bob said.
"Gosh, no! I just don't like
my pumpkins disappearing.
Hand me the nails, please?"

Stanley passed Uncle Bob some nails.

Uncle Bob fixed

the scarecrow's shoulder.

"I've tried standing guard at night,

but the thieves just wait

until I go home," he said.

Stanley looked at the scarecrow's

skinny wooden arm.

Then he looked at his own flat one.

"Uncle Bob, I have a plan."

That night the moon lit the sky.

Stanley stood still,

trying not to scratch.

It was hard, since his sleeves

and pants were stuffed with straw!

Stanley was about to give in

and scratch when he saw something.

Two flashlights bobbing in the dark!

"This way!" a voice whispered.

The lights grew closer.

Stanley held his breath.

Then someone bumped right into him!

"Ow! This scarecrow's elbow
is so pointy!" said the thief.

"Gotcha!" Stanley yelled.

Then he snatched the flashlight

and shone it in both thieves' faces.

"WHAT on EARTH?" Stanley said.

"Arthur and Billy,

why are you stealing pumpkins?"

"It's a surprise for Uncle Bob,"

Arthur said.

"Some surprise!" said Stanley.

"No, really!" said Billy.

"The fair's tomorrow.

Dad's too shy to take his pumpkins,

but I know he could win a prize.

Arthur's helping me find good ones.

We're going to show them at the fair!"

Stanley couldn't help smiling.

"That really is a good surprise.

How can I help?"

"Well, there's one thing you can do . . ."
said Arthur.

Uncle Bob found Stanley the next day.

"Did the thieves show up last night?"

"Oh, yes," said Stanley. "Come see."

"WHAT on EARTH?" Uncle Bob said.

The boys quickly explained the plan.

"Arthur and I will handle everything!
You can just watch," said Billy.
"What do you say, Dad?"

"Well, gosh," said Uncle Bob.
"It looks like my pumpkins
are going to the fair!"

That afternoon, they all celebrated

Uncle Bob's first-ever blue ribbon!

Uncle Bob couldn't stop grinning.

"This is so exciting!

Thank you, boys!"

"I know just the thing to do
with this prizewinning pumpkin,"
said Aunt Sue.

"Make a prizewinning pie!

Stanley, you MUST eat another slice. . . ."